Other books by Raymond Briggs

Jim and the Beanstalk
The Fairy Tale Treasury
The Elephant and the Bad Baby (text by Elfrida Vipont)
Father Christmas Goes on Holiday
Father Christmas – Having a Wonderful Time
Fungus the Bogeyman
The Snowman
The Snowman Story Book
The Snowman Soft-and-Small Baby Book
The Snowman Tell-the-Time Book
The Snowman Touch-and-Feel Book
The Snowman (Miniature Edition)
Father Christmas (Miniature Edition)

FATHER CHRISTMAS

RAYMOND BRIGGS
Father Christmas

Random House New York

For my Mother and Father

Copyright © 1973 by Raymond Briggs.
All rights reserved under International and Pan-American Copyright Conventions.
Published in the United States by Random House, Inc., New York.
Originally published in Great Britain by Hamish Hamilton, Ltd., London, in 1973.
http://www.randomhouse.com/
Library of Congress Cataloging-in-Publication Data
Briggs, Raymond. Father christmas / Raymond Briggs. p. cm. SUMMARY: A rather grumpy
Father Christmas delivers gifts on Christmas Eve.
ISBN 0-679-88776-8 (hardcover)
1. Santa Claus—Juvenile Fiction. [1. Santa Claus—Fiction. 2. Christmas—Fiction.]
I. Title. PZ7.B7646Fat 1997 [E]—dc21 96-5667
Printed in Italy 10 9 8 7 6 5 4 3 2 1

Father Christmas

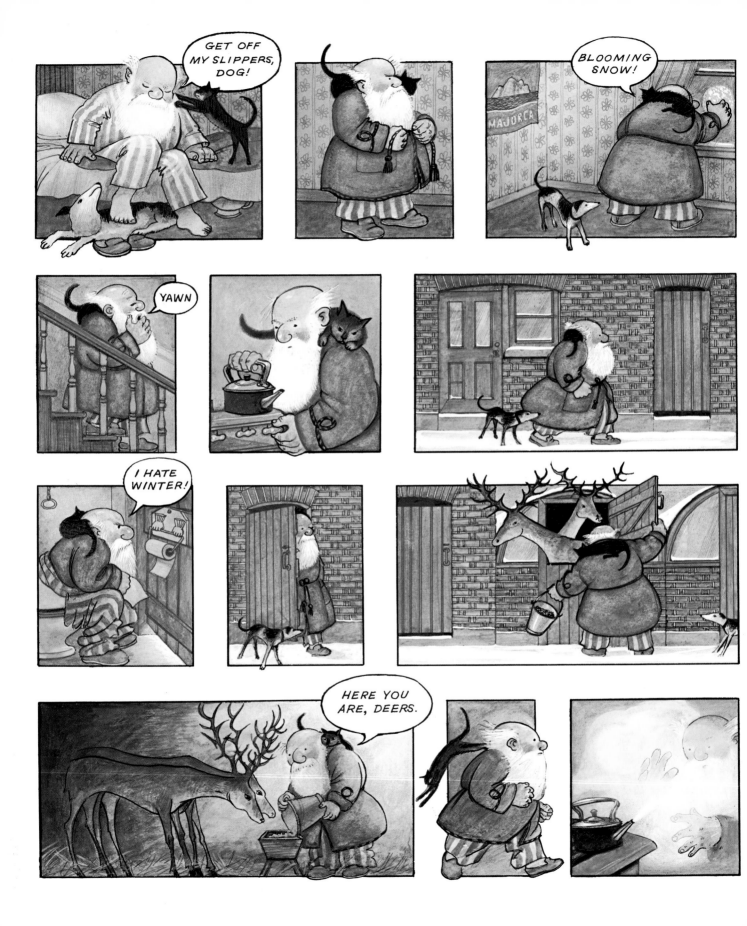

KEEP STILL YOU SILLY DEERS!

GOODBYE
CAT

GOODBYE
DOG

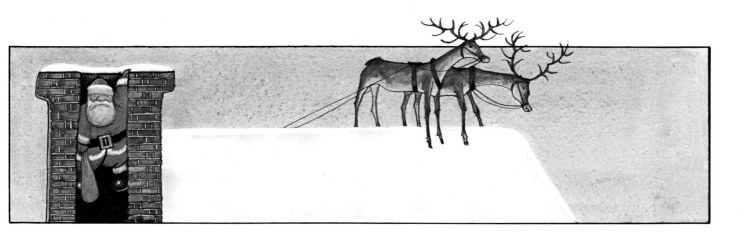

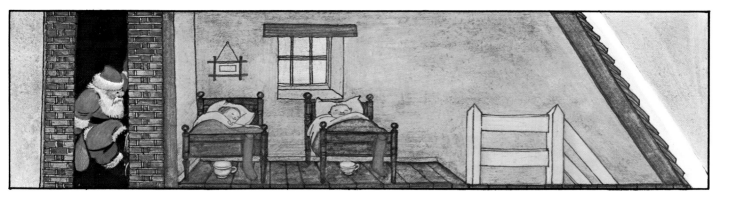

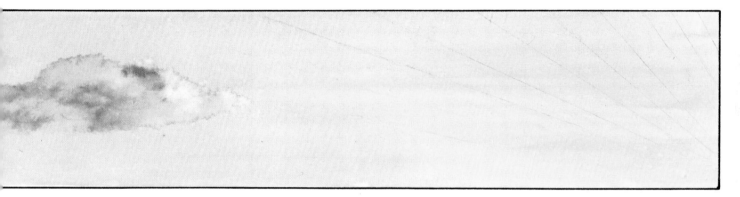

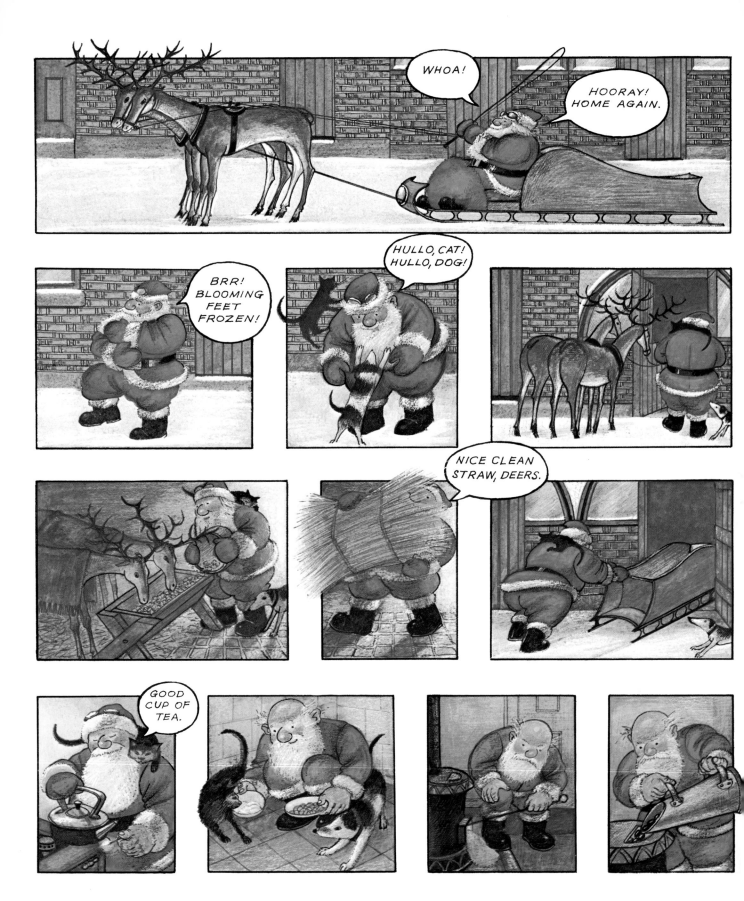

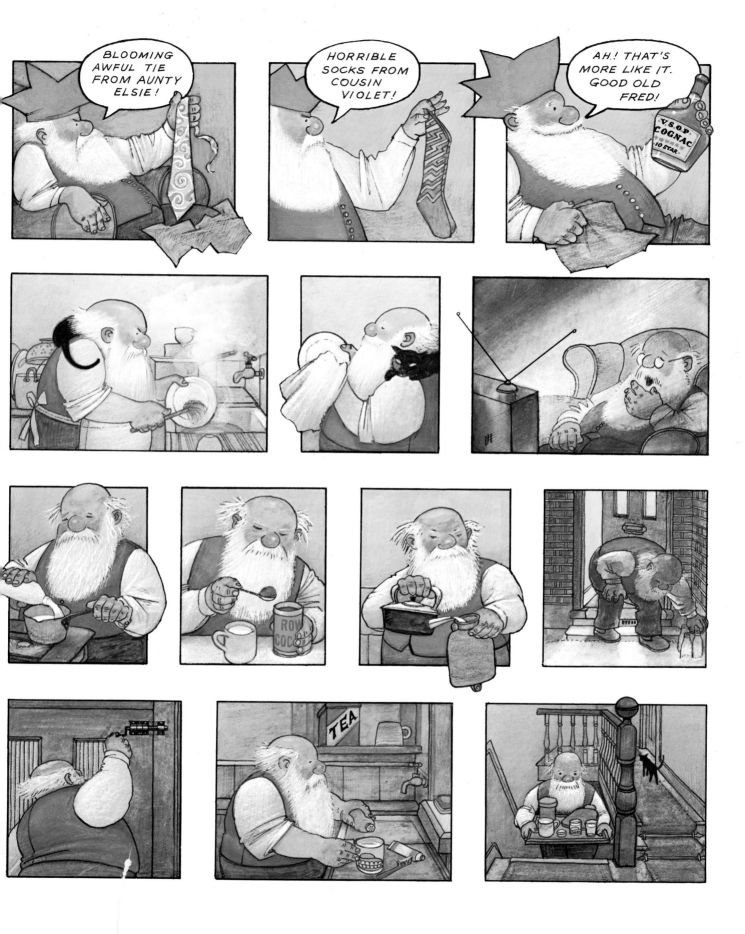

The End